Ann Grifalconi

Ain't Nobody a Stranger to Me

ILLUSTRATED BY

Jerry Pinkney

JUMP AT THE SUN
HYPERION BOOKS FOR CHILDREN
New York

For information address Hyperion Books for Children,
114 Fifth Avenue, New York, New York 10011-5690.

Printed in Hong Kong
First Edition
1 3 5 7 9 10 8 6 4 2
Reinforced binding
This book is set in Cloister.

Library of Congress Cataloging-in-Publication Data on file.
ISBN-13: 978-0-7868-1857-0
ISBN-10: 0-7868-1857-3
Visit www.jumpatthesun.com

To all helping hearts!
—*A. G.*

To Charles L. Blockson—keeper of the flame
—*J. P.*

ALONG, LONG TIME AGO, when I was a little, little girl, my Gran'pa let me come along on his weekly visit to his apple orchard. "It's the last piece of land I kept," he told me, waving his hand in a friendly "hello" at every passerby, "after I moved into town."

"Gran'pa!" I called, running to keep up with him. "How come you know so many people?"

He stopped to let me catch up. "Don't know 'em by name—just by heart, Honey. . . . *Ain't nobody a stranger to me!*"

"Why's that, Gran'pa?" I asked, grabbing his hand in mine and holding on.

He grinned happily down at me. "'Cause both me and my heart is free."

After a while of walking, he asked me: "Did you know, Honey, that way back in the sad, old days of slavery, I used to carry apple seeds in my pockets, to keep myself believing that when the great day of freedom came, I could plant 'em in my own soil, on my own farm?"

I shook my head. I did not know.

"But finally, one day it came to me," Gran'pa
went on. "It weren't never gonna happen 'til we
struck out for freedom ourselves!

"So we got ready . . . and the first night we
could, we run away!"

"Who's 'we,' Gran'pa?"

"It was me, your Gran'ma Polly, and our baby girl—that's your mama," Gran'pa said, tousling my curly hair. "'Course we was afraid. But we was careful, quiet, sure of foot."

He stopped walking, remembering how it was. . . .

"Now, we had already come a long way north, dodging strangers and dangers all the way.

"We was coming close to the Ohio River, close to freedom! But bein' too tired an' hungry to go another step, we picked us out a barn nearby to hide inside.

"We slept there real quiet all that night—baby, too. Then at dawn, this man came down to the barn to milk his cows. And wouldn't you know—just then, the baby cried out!

"We stood in the dark, arms tight around our hungry baby—so desperate, we was ready to run and swim the Ohio to freedom on the other side—die if we had to!

"We wasn't goin' back!"

"Oh, no!" I said, shivering at the thought, though I knew my Gran'daddy was safe here with me. I hugged his hand even tighter!

"'Course, even in the dark," Gran'pa added, "the man felt somebody was there. But guess what?"

I looked up at him, still full of worry.

"That man sure didn't see no color then! Only saw we was in trouble. The man was white, but he did right by us that day!

"And he never asked my name, though he told me his: James Stanton. Turns out he was a secret member of the Underground Railroad!"

"Oh!" I shouted. "Those folks who helped the runaways travel north?"

"Yep! The folks who helped lift us up when we was down. The Quaker James Stanton and his wife, Sarah, never said, 'That's no white baby! That's only a brown baby.' To them, she was just a hungry little child.

"And so they fed us and helped us cross the river to freedom the very next night!"

"That sure was lucky for you, Gran'pa!" I said, feeling safer now, my hand resting in his.

"Don't know if it was luck, Hon." He shook his head. "We had to put our trust in the Good Lord. We'd set our hearts right, and all along the way help came when we needed it. And we got through. Yes, we got through. . . ."

"Yep." Gran'pa nodded. "I been on both sides. When somebody falls down, what kind of man gonna stop 'n' say: 'I don't pick up no stranger! Let 'em lie there'? Leastways, not me!"

We walked together in silence.

Soon, the spring air began to carry the fresh, sweet smell of apple blossoms to us.

"Once we got north of south," Gran'pa continued, walking faster, "me 'n' Polly worked hard and long, hiring ourselves out as paid labor—blacksmithin', plowin', sewin', pickin' apples, milkin' cows—'til we put aside enough to buy ourselves some land of our own—right here!

"And here it is!" Gran'pa beamed proudly as we came to a whole pink cloud of blooming apple trees. "Remember those seeds I carried with me?

"Well, I took those seeds and put 'em into our own soil. An' every time I planted one, I thought of someone who'd helped us on our way. . . . And now we seein' the blossoms!"

Now Gran'pa was pulling an apple from each pocket.

"They be from our stone cellar, Grandpa?"

"Yep. Saved these to eat here with you, Honey!"

And we both sat down and munched away.

"Could I, Gran'pa," I asked, "could I one day plant me a seed of memory here, too?"

Gran'pa laughed, touched. "Right now would be just fine!"

Then he watched as I planted new seeds in the family orchard from the apple I had just eaten.

I could tell he was remembering, too. . . . .

"I won't forget you did this, Honey." Gran'pa smiled as we walked away.

I put my hand on my chest. "I won't forget what you said, Gran'pa—not ever!"

I knew I never would.

"And so now you see why"—Gran'pa paused, and I saw such joy rising in his face as he waved hello to heaven—*"Ain't nobody a stranger to me!"*